DATE DUE		

The Urbana Free Library

To renew: call 217-367-4057
or go to "*urbanafreelibrary.org*"
and select "Renew/Request Items"

Banana Spaghetti was not the way I had imagined it.

It wasn't yellow. It was brown. It wasn't happy. It looked miserable.

It looked worse than turnips, worse than eggplant, worse than a baked fish eye.

"Maybe it's better than we think," Julian said. "When you don't like some stuff, Mom always tells you it's better than you think."

"Will she eat it?" I asked.

"She'll eat it because we made it," Julian said.

"That might not be a good enough reason," I said.

Julian, Huey, and Gloria books by Ann Cameron

The Stories Julian Tells
More Stories Julian Tells
Julian's Glorious Summer
Julian, Secret Agent
Julian, Dream Doctor
The Stories Huey Tells
More Stories Huey Tells
Gloria Rising

The Stories Huey Tells

by Ann Cameron
illustrated by Roberta Smith

A STEPPING STONE BOOK™
Random House New York

Copyright © 1995 by Ann Cameron
Illustrations copyright © 1995 by Roberta Smith

All rights reserved. Published in the United States by Random House Children's Books, a division of Random House, Inc., New York. Originally published in hardcover by Alfred A. Knopf, an imprint of Random House Children's Books, a division of Random House, Inc., New York, in 1995.

RANDOM HOUSE and colophon are registered trademarks and A STEPPING STONE BOOK and colophon are trademarks of Random House, Inc.

www.steppingstonesbooks.com
www.randomhouse.com/kids

Educators and librarians, for a variety of teaching tools, visit us at
www.randomhouse.com/teachers

Reprinted by arrangement with Alfred A. Knopf, an imprint of Random House Children's Books, a division of Random House, Inc., New York.

Cover illustration copyright © Robert Papp

Library of Congress Cataloging-in-Publication Data
Cameron, Ann.
The stories Huey tells / by Ann Cameron ; illustrated by Roberta Smith.
   p. cm. — "A Stepping Stone book."
SUMMARY: Huey shows big brother Julian that he's an adventurer, a chef,
a tracker, and a scout.
ISBN-13: 978-0-679-88559-7 (trade) — ISBN-13: 978-0-679-96732-3 (lib. bdg.)
ISBN-10: 0-679-88559-5 (trade) — ISBN-10: 0-679-96732-X (lib. bdg.)
[1. Brothers—Fiction. 2. Family life—Fiction. 3. African Americans—Fiction.]
I. Smith, Roberta, ill. II. Title.
PZ7.C1427Sr 2006   [Fic]—dc22   2006008762

Printed in the United States of America   24 23 22 21 20

Contents

Blue Light, Green Light

My brother, Julian, isn't scared of the dark. Nighttime doesn't bother him. He just gets into bed, puts a pillow over his head, and goes to sleep.

Not me. I don't like the dark, and I get scary dreams. One I dreamed lots of times, and every time I dreamed it, it got worse. Finally I told it to Julian.

"I was walking in a high place. Then all of a sudden I went over a cliff. The whole world just dissolved. I was falling straight down to the bottom of the universe. I was going to hit it and die."

"Then what?" Julian asked.

"I woke up."

"That's nothing!" Julian said. "I've had much scarier dreams than that! Once I dreamed a lion licked my face. But I wasn't even scared!"

"A lion is not like falling!" I said. He made me mad. He always acts like nothing I say is important.

"It's no use telling you anything!" I said.

I told my mom my dream—how when I was falling, it was like my stomach climbed up into my head.

She said maybe the dream wouldn't happen anymore if my body had more calcium. She said she'd fix me warm milk with honey before I went to bed.

I told my dad my dream.

"I was falling through nowhere," I said. "There wasn't one solid thing anywhere! And I just kept dropping faster and faster all the way to the bottom of the universe."

"Huey," my dad said, "the universe doesn't have a bottom. So you can't hit it. And there isn't any *nowhere!* Everyplace is *somewhere.*"

"In the dream, it's like I'm paralyzed. And it seems like I'm nowhere."

"Maybe your mattress is too soft," my dad said. "I'll put a piece of plywood under it."

And he did. But the next night, even with calcium and plywood, I was falling just the same.

"Plywood didn't fix it," I told my dad.

"I still feel like I'm falling through nowhere."

He had just come home from work. "Give me time to think," he said.

He went into the house and sat in his favorite chair. He put his elbows on his knees and his chin in his hands. He shut his eyes and pulled his hair. He sighed.

Then he opened his eyes and smiled.

"I have just what you need in the basement!" he said.

He ran down the basement stairs and came up with something in a bag.

"Come on!" he said.

We went straight upstairs to my bed. He reached into the bag like a magician.

"*This* is the answer!" he said.

He pulled out a brand-new brick.

"How is that going to help me?" I asked.

"Feel it!" Dad said.

I felt it.

"This brick," my dad said, "is solid."

He set it down in the middle of my bed.

"Now," he said, "try it."

"*Try* it?" I said.

"Yes," he said. "Lie down on it!"

"Lie *down* on it?!" I said.

"Yes!" he said.

I didn't really want to try it, but I did. I lay back. I could feel the edges of the brick against my spine. I could even feel the three round holes in the middle of it. I sat up.

"How did it feel, Huey?" my dad asked.

"Hard!" I said.

"See!" my dad said. "That's how the world really is. Hard! Full of hard stuff.

You really *can't* just fall away to nowhere. If you sleep on this nice new brick, it will tell your body that!"

"Dad," I said, "if I lie on that brick, I will never sleep again!"

My dad looked disappointed.

"Anyhow," he said, "maybe your body will remember how it felt and not forget the world is solid. Or, if you wake up, maybe just touching it will help."

He put it next to the lamp on my night table.

"What's that?" Julian asked when he saw it.

"It's a present from Dad," I said.

"Why didn't he give *me* a present?" Julian asked.

"You don't need one," I said.

When I woke up at night, I touched the brick. It made me feel better, but it didn't stop my bad dream.

Julian and I have a friend, Gloria. I was scared to tell her about my dream. I was scared she'd nothing it, like Julian. But one day when Julian wasn't around, I told her anyway.

"That's a horrible dream!" she said. She sounded like she really understood how it was. Even though she was understanding a horrible thing, her understanding made me feel good.

"Do you get scary dreams?" I asked.

"Sometimes," she said. "Real bad ones."

And she told me about them.

The worst was about some bad guys

with guns trying to break down the door to her house. She and her mom and dad pushed and pushed against the door to hold the bad guys back. And then the door broke, and she and her folks started running.

But they couldn't run fast enough...

"That dream is as bad as mine!" I said.

"Yes!" Gloria said. "And when I wake up, I feel scared and kind of sick to my stomach. And I don't want to go back to sleep. I can be brave when I'm awake—but it's hard to be brave when you're asleep."

"I wish we could signal each other when we wake up at night," I said. "So we could tell each other that we are okay."

"With lights in our bedroom windows, we could do it," Gloria said. "I could see yours shining, and you could see mine."

"We should do it," I said.

So we asked our folks for permission to buy lights and hang them in our windows. Gloria's folks said she could do it if I could. My folks said I had to ask Julian.

I thought he would say no. But he didn't. He said it was a good idea.

My dad drove us to a hardware store. We bought reflector lights with strong clamps and colored reflector bulbs. Gloria bought a green bulb. Julian and I bought a blue one.

My dad let the three of us out of the truck at Gloria's house. The clamp on the light was hard to open. Gloria's mom and dad clamped it to the windowsill for her. Gloria screwed in the bulb and plugged in the light. It worked!

At our house we got our light fixed up just like Gloria's, and Gloria stayed for supper. Afterward, she went home so we could test our signals.

Julian and I went up to our room. Exactly at nine, we screwed in the bulb. Our blue light shone out. Down the street there came an answer—a green light glowing in Gloria's window.

"It works!" Julian said. "And it isn't quite so dark in here. Sometimes it gets *too* dark. That's why I sleep with a pillow over my head."

I was surprised. "I thought you *liked* the dark," I said.

"A whole lot of it is too much," Julian said.

I thought. Maybe it wasn't just me and Gloria that didn't like the dark. Maybe it scares everybody a little.

"If it gets too dark," I told him, "you can come and get in bed with me sometimes."

And now, sometimes he does.

There's one good thing about the dark.

In daylight our signals don't show up. It's the dark that makes them beautiful.

I don't have falling dreams anymore. I don't know why. Maybe the reason is the plywood. Maybe it's my brick. Maybe it's hot milk with honey. Maybe it's because I know everybody is scared sometimes.

Now when I wake up at night, there's a blue glow in our room. I know our light is shining strong to Gloria's house. I get up and go to the window. Beyond lots of dark houses I see Gloria's green light. It is steady and bright, like a beam from a lighthouse that guides ships away from danger.

I know from her house, ours is that bright too. I stand a long time at the

window looking out from our light to hers, feeling happy.

We are okay. Me, and Julian, and Gloria.

The Rule

My mom and dad have a rule. At every meal, Julian and I have to eat at least a little bit of everything on our plates.

Julian doesn't mind. My mom says that ever since he was a baby he liked to eat every single vegetable and all kinds of strange foods.

When I was born, my mom thought that I would be like Julian. I'm not. It's because of me that they made up the rule.

Because of the rule, I have eaten a little bit of oysters and asparagus. I have eaten a little bit of eggplant and turnips.

I have eaten a piece of radish so tiny that afterward I had to use a magnifying glass to show my parents there was something missing from that radish.

Because of the radish, they added to the rule. You cannot use a magnifying glass to prove you tasted something. You have to eat more of it than that.

There is one other part to the rule. It is about restaurants. That part is:

Food in restaurants is expensive. In a restaurant, if you order something, you better eat it *all*.

One day my mom and dad decided to take me and Julian out for dinner. They invited Gloria to come too.

My mom told us to dress up for the restaurant, with dark pants and white shirts and our best Sunday shoes. Julian tried to dress to look grown up.

I was worried about the rule. I tried to dress the best way for getting hungry. I fastened the belt on my best pants very tight. I hoped that would make me hungry.

We stopped and picked up Gloria, who was all dressed up too. She had on a pink dress and new shoes with bows on them.

The name of the restaurant was King Henry's. There were lots of cars parked out front, and there was a red carpet leading inside. A man as dressed up as us opened the door and took us to a table.

Our waiter was very tall and thin. He looked like he could eat ten dinners at once and they would just disappear inside him. He probably knew the right way to wear his belt for getting hungry.

When he brought us menus, I scrinched my neck around so I could see his belt. It was very loose! I loosened mine three notches. Right away I felt hungry.

The menu was in a leather holder. It was very big, with fancy gold and black writing. I looked for words I knew. A little card was pinned right in the middle of the first page:

Special

Grilled Giant Forest Mushrooms with Fresh Trout from Cold Mountain Rivers

---

"Special" is my favorite word. I also like the words "giant," "fresh," and "rivers." The words made me very hungry. I loosened my belt one more notch.

"What's trout?" I asked my mom.

"It's a fish," she said.

"That's what I want," I said.

"Are you sure?" my dad asked. "Are you sure you don't want a hamburger?

That's what Julian's having. Or maybe
you'd like the chef's salad? That's what
Gloria's having."

"I'm sure," I said. "I want the Special."

"You know you'll have to eat it when it comes," my mom said.

"I will," I said.

The thin man brought Julian's hamburger, Gloria's salad, and my mom and dad's chicken. He brought me the Special.

The giant mushrooms were all around the plate, just like a forest. The trout was in the middle. He still wore his skin and his head. His mouth was open as if he was gasping for air. His eye was big and white and sad and cooked. It looked right straight at me.

"Sorry," I said. I looked away.

I looked at the giant mushrooms. Their tops were like wings. They looked like a dark forest. They were a little mushy, but

they still looked like rooms. Probably elves
had lived under them and danced around
them in the moonlight. If I ate one, I could
be eating an elf's house.

But I had to do it. "Sorry," I said.

I took my knife and fork. I cut myself
a bite. It tasted like a buttered forest. I

liked the taste. I ate all my mushrooms.

"Huey ate *all* his mushrooms!" my mom said.

"But," my dad said, "he hasn't touched his fish."

"I will," I said.

I didn't want to touch it with my finger. I touched the tail with my knife.

The eye of the fish looked at me. I stopped touching its tail.

I wondered if I was supposed to eat the eye. If I had to, I would eat the tail first. I would save the eye till last.

I could eat the fish if I didn't look at it.

But it is hard to eat your food if you don't look at it. You keep missing the plate with your fork.

There were mirrors on two sides of the

room. I could see my fork miss the plate
two ways. I could see the heaps of salad
left on Gloria's plate.

"Mrs. Bates," Gloria said, "do you mind
if I don't eat all my salad?"

"Of course not, honey," my mom said.
"You're a guest."

I turned around in my chair and looked
at the back of the room. There was an
aquarium! It was full of purple fish, live
ones with frilly tails like ballerinas' dresses.
They were watching me. It looked like
they were talking to each other. They
wanted to see what I would do.

"Sorry," I muttered to the purple fish.
I put my fork in my lap.

"Huey," my dad said, "we're almost
done."

"Sorry," I said.

"You don't have to eat the head or the tail or the skin," my mom explained. "Just break the skin open and eat the flesh."

"Flesh!" I said.

"Meat," my mom said.

"Huey—if you finish your fish, you can have ice cream," my dad promised.

I moved my legs. My fork slipped out of my lap and so did my napkin. Right away the thin man saw. He picked them up and took them away. Then he put a clean fork by my plate. He handed me a fresh napkin.

I remembered something I saw once on TV—a live heart operation. The doctors didn't look at the patient. They kept him covered up with a cloth. My mom said they did it so they could forget he was a person and cut.

I took my fresh napkin and threw it over my whole fish, all but the middle.

Julian almost choked on a piece of bread. "Huey's napkin!" he said, pointing.

"Yuck!" Gloria said. "Huey!" my dad exclaimed. "Your manners!" my mom reminded.

I didn't listen. There wasn't time.

I picked up my fork. I took a big chunk out of my fish's side, and chewed it, and swallowed it.

I swallowed three times extra for safety. I ate nine more big bites.

"Huey ate almost all of it," Gloria said.

"Huey has to eat it *all*," Julian said. "That's the rule!"

I looked at Mom and Dad. "Do I have to?" I said. I felt awfully full.

"Julian," my mom said, "rules aren't absolute. People make rules to make life better. If a rule doesn't work, it can be changed."

My dad said, "Huey ate a lot of good food tonight. If he eats more, he might burst."

My mom said, "I'm proud of Huey. He ate two new foods. He was adventurous."

It sounded like I was a hero. An explorer maybe.

"But what about the rule?" Julian protested.

"Maybe we don't even need it anymore," my mom said. "What do you think, Huey?"

I looked at my plate. The mushrooms were all gone. I'd eaten almost all the fish. Julian never ever ate that much. If he ever tried it in a restaurant, he could never do it.

"Let's keep the rule," I said.

Chef Huey

Food should be different from the way it is," I said to my mom. "Then I wouldn't mind eating it."

"How should it be different?" my mom asked.

"I don't exactly know," I said.

"Maybe you will figure it out and be a chef," my mom said.

"What's a chef?" I asked.

"A chef is a very good cook who some-times invents new things to eat," my mom told me.

The next day we went to the super-market. I saw pictures of chefs on some of the food packages. They were all smil-ing. I wondered if when they were little they had to eat what their parents told them to eat. Maybe that's why they became chefs—so they could invent foods that they liked to eat. Probably that's when they became happy.

The chef with the biggest smile of all was Chef Marco on the can of Chef Marco's Spaghetti.

"Please get that can," I said to my mom. "I want to take it home."

I wanted to invent something with it, but I wasn't sure what.

At first I couldn't think of anything it went with. Instead, I thought of cakes like pillows. I thought of carrots that would be fastened together around meat loaf to make skyscrapers. One night I did tie some carrots around a meat loaf my dad made— but the strings that fastened them came loose in the oven, and the skyscraper fell down.

It was the night before Mother's Day when I thought of a brand-new food.

I could see it in my mind. Something yellow. A happy yellow food. One that didn't mind being eaten.

In the morning, Julian and I were going to bring my mom breakfast in bed. Julian was going to fry eggs. I told him I had a better idea.

"What is it?" he asked.

"Banana Spaghetti," I said.

"Banana Spaghetti!" he said. "I never heard of it!"

"It's a new invention!" I said. "It will be a one hundred percent surprise."

Julian likes surprises. "So how do we make it?" he asked.

"Simple!" I said. "We have bananas and we have spaghetti. All we have to do is put them together."

Julian thought about it. "We'd better get up early tomorrow," he said. "Just in case."

At 6 A.M. we went downstairs very quietly and turned on the lights in the kitchen. We went to work.

We mashed up three ripe bananas. I took out the can of Chef Marco's Spaghetti. In the picture on the can, Chef Marco had his arms spread out wide, with a steaming platter balanced above his head on one hand.

I decided to stand that way when I brought Mom the Banana Spaghetti. I would go up the stairs ahead of Julian with her plate, so Julian couldn't take all the credit.

I held the can and Julian opened it. We put the spaghetti in a bowl. It had a lot of tomato sauce on it—the color of blood.

"We have to get the tomato off!" I said.

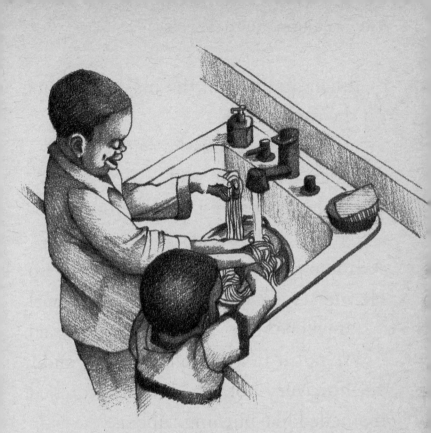

We put the spaghetti in the sink and washed it with hot water. It got nice and clean. We put it on a platter.

"It looks kind of spongy," Julian said.

"It will be good," I said. "We just need to put the sauce on it."

Julian dumped all the mashed banana on the top.

"Banana Spaghetti!" I said.

"Taste it!" Julian said.

But I wasn't sure I wanted to.

"You try it!" I said.

Julian tasted it. His lips puckered up. He wiped his mouth with a kitchen towel.

"It will be better when it's hot," he said.

We put it in a pan on the stove and it got hot. Very hot. The banana scorched. It smelled like burning rubber.

Julian turned off the stove. We looked into the pan.

"Not all of it burned," Julian said. "Just the bottom. We can put the rest on the plates."

We did. Then we looked at it.

Banana Spaghetti was not the way I had imagined it. It wasn't yellow. It was brown. It wasn't happy. It looked miserable.

It looked worse than turnips, worse than eggplant, worse than a baked fish eye.

"Maybe it's better than we think," Julian said. "When you don't like some stuff, Mom always tells you it's better than you think."

"Will she eat it?" I asked.

"She'll eat it because we made it," Julian said.

"That might not be a good enough reason," I said.

"You can tell her just to *try* a little bit," Julian advised.

That seemed like a good idea. "Let's take it upstairs," I said. I handed Mom's plate to him.

"No," Julian said. "You take it up. It's your invention." He handed the plate back to me.

I put the plate on a tray with a knife and a fork and a napkin. I started up the stairs. I tried holding the tray above my head on one hand, but it was very tippy. I couldn't do it the way Chef Marco did. And I wasn't happy like Chef Marco, either. I wished Julian was with me.

I climbed five steps. *It's better than you think,* I told myself.

On the sixth step I just sat down with the tray in my lap and stayed there.

I heard the door to my folks' room open. I heard feet hurrying down the stairs. My dad's.

He stopped when he saw me.

"Huey," he said, "what are you doing?"

"Thinking," I said. "What are *you* doing?"

"Going for coffee—what is that stuff you're holding?"

"It's Banana Spaghetti," I said. "I invented it. Julian and I made it for Mom. We thought it would be good. But it didn't come out the way I wanted it to."

My dad sat by me and looked at it. I passed it to him.

"It does seem to have a problem," he said. "Maybe several problems."

He sniffed it and wrinkled his nose. He got a faraway, professional look on his face, as if he was comparing it with all the banana foods he had ever tasted in his life. He looked as wise as Chef Marco.

"Banana Spaghetti," he said. "It's a good idea. You just need to make it differently."

"How?"

"Spaghetti is usually made of flour and eggs," Dad explained. "But I think we could make it from flour and banana. After I have my coffee, we can try."

We went to the kitchen. Julian had eggs out. He was getting a frying pan.

"You can put that frying pan away, Julian," my dad said. "We're making Banana Spaghetti."

He flicked the switch on the coffee maker. In a minute coffee spurted out, and he poured himself a cup and sipped it.

"I'm ready," he said. "Peel me three bananas, boys!"

We did.

"Now put them in this bowl and mash them!" he said.

We did. They came out sort of white, just like the first ones we mashed. And flour wasn't going to change the color.

"Dad," I said, "I want Banana Spaghetti to be yellow. It's not going to be yellow, is it?"

"Not without help," my dad said. "Look in the cupboard. Maybe there's some yellow food coloring in there."

We took everything out of the cupboard. Toothpicks, napkins, salt, burn ointment, cans of soup, instant coffee,

six pennies, and a spider web. At the very back I found a tiny bottle of yellow stuff. I showed it to my dad.

"That's it!" he said. "Put some in, Huey! Just a few drops."

I did.

"Stir that yellow around," he said.

We took spoons and did it.

"Bring me the flour," he said.

We did.

He dumped some in the bowl.

"This is tough to mix," my dad said, "so let me do it."

With a fork he mixed the flour and banana into a dough.

"Julian! Spread some flour on this counter!" he said.

Julian did.

My dad set the dough on the floured counter. "I have to knead this dough," he said. "You boys clean the cupboard and put everything back in it."

We did, except for the pennies. We asked if we could have them, and my dad said yes. We put them in our pockets.

Dad rolled up the sleeves of his pajamas and pushed the dough back and forth under his hands, twisting and turning and pressing it hard, until it was smooth and not sticky.

"The dough has to rest so it will be stretchy," he said. He covered it with an upside-down bowl and put a big pot of water on the stove to boil.

"What should go in the sauce?" he asked. "It's your invention, Huey, so you decide."

I tried to think of the best ingredient in the world.

"What about—whipped cream?" I asked. I never had any spaghetti that way, but I thought it would be good.

"Whipped cream! A great idea!" my dad said.

I poured cream into a bowl. Dad got the electric mixer out, and I beat the cream.

"How about—sugar?" Julian said.

"Sugar is right," I said. Julian poured some in.

"Now," my dad said, "what about spices? How about—oregano?" And he gave me the oregano bottle so I could smell it.

It smelled like pizza. "No!" I said.

"How about—cinnamon?" he asked.

Julian and I both smelled the cinnamon. "Yes!" we said.

"And how about—ginger?" He handed me the can.

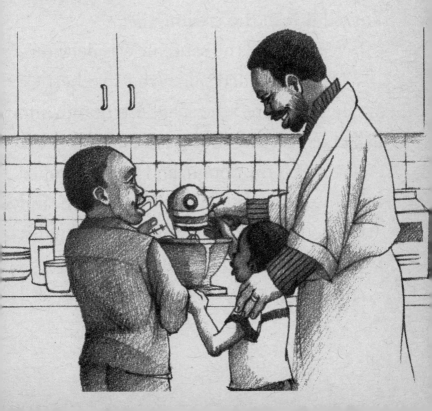

Julian and I both smelled it. Julian said no. I said yes. Banana Spaghetti is mine, so I won. My dad shook in some ginger, and then he beat the cream till it was thick and fluffy.

"How about—sliced banana?" Julian asked.

I said yes. We sliced a banana. My dad stirred it into the cream.

We all tasted the sauce. It was delicious.

"Now," my dad said, "the spaghetti."

He uncovered the spaghetti dough and asked us for the rolling pin and the flour.

He rolled the dough, and then we rolled it some. Finally, when it was thin and stretched out like a blanket, he folded it over two times and cut it into strips.

Julian and I separated the strips and

unfolded them. They were long and smooth and yellow. We held them in our hands gently, like Christmas tree tinsel.

The water in the pot was boiling as if it wanted to jump out. We stood on chairs by the stove and dropped in all the spaghetti strings at once. They sunk and swam in the pot for just a minute before my dad dipped in a fork and fished one out.

He tasted it.

"Done!" he said. "Quick! Get the plates ready!"

We did. Dad set a strainer in the sink. He poured everything out of the pot. All the water washed down the drain. The spaghetti stayed in the strainer. He divided the spaghetti on the plates and shook some cinnamon over it. I spread the sauce on top. It looked good— except for one thing.

"Just a minute!" I said. I found a bag of chopped peanuts and tossed some on top of each plate of Banana Spaghetti.

"Is that everything, Huey?" my dad said.

"Yes," I said.

"Delivery time!" Julian said.

I went first with two plates. Julian came behind me with the other two plates. My dad came last, with silverware, coffee, and orange juice on a tray.

My hands were full. I knocked on the bedroom door with the edge of one plate.

"Come in!" my mom said. I hoped she would be just waking, but she was sitting up in bed, reading a book. She looked hungry.

I set one plate on the bureau. I brought the other to her the way Chef Marco would have done it, held out like a gift.

"Happy Mother's Day!" I said.

"What *is* this?" she said.

"Just—Banana Spaghetti," I said.

My dad handed her a fork. She tasted it.

"Delicious!" she said. "Very strange, but *very* delicious."

"Dad and Julian helped me," I said. "But it's my invention."

We arranged everything so we could all eat on the bed. When we had eaten all the spaghetti, we had second helpings of sauce.

My mom scooped up the last bit of her sauce with a spoon. "Banana Spaghetti! What a wonderful breakfast!" she said.

And I was very proud. Just yesterday there was no such thing as Banana Spaghetti in the whole world—and now there is. Just like one time the telephone didn't exist, or television, or space stations. A lot of people believed those things could never exist. But then some great inventor made them.

I am an inventor. And a chef.

And I know what I want for dinner on

my birthday. Banana Spaghetti. With chocolate shavings over the sauce, and seven yellow candles on the top.

Tracks

Julian had a book from the library. By reading the book, he was learning to be a tracker and a guide and a scout. He had shown it to Gloria. He wouldn't show it to me.

"I could learn too," I said.

"You couldn't!" Julian said.

"I could too!" I said.

Julian shook his head. "A tracker is strong and silent. You're too little—and you talk all the time."

I hate it when Julian acts like that. It makes me want to fight him. But I didn't say one word. I just went away.

In the night I woke up and went downstairs. Julian's book was lying on the couch in the living room. I picked it up. I couldn't read it all, but I could see it was about tracks.

It had pictures of the hoof and paw prints of almost every kind of animal. It showed deer tracks and raccoon tracks, the tracks of zebras and giraffes and elephants.

I looked out the living room window. I could hear the wind. I could almost hear many animals outside. Very quietly I opened the front door and went out. I still had the book in my hand.

There was a full moon. I could see my own shadow on the grass, but I couldn't see any night animals. I looked for tracks, but there weren't any.

In real life I really had seen raccoon tracks once. I looked through Julian's book until I found some. I decided to copy them. I found a sharp stick and went to where our driveway divides our lawn in two parts. The driveway isn't paved. It's pebbly and sandy.

Raccoon tracks look almost like human

hands, with narrow fingers and long, sharp claws for fingernails. I stood on the grass and used my stick to copy them along the edge of the driveway.

I walked on the grass to the street. Then I walked on the paved street to the other side of our driveway. I copied more raccoon tracks on that side—so it looked like the raccoon had turned around and gone back to the street.

I hid my drawing stick in the hedge and went back in the house. I was careful not to leave any footprints. I put Julian's book back on the couch, just the way he'd left it. I climbed the stairs, tiptoed past Mom and Dad's room, and went back to bed.

In the morning I went down to breakfast. Julian was running into the kitchen with his book in his hand.

"Dad! Dad!" he shouted. "A raccoon was here last night!"

"Really?" my dad said. He went outside with Julian to study the tracks, and I went along.

Julian showed Dad his book. When Dad bent down to look at the tracks, I tried to look at Julian's book too. But Julian wouldn't let me. Whenever I tried to, he covered it with his arm and poked me in the ribs with his elbow.

My dad stood up. "It sure does look like a raccoon was here!" he said. "Sometimes those little rascals come round to eat food out of garbage cans. From now on, we'll need to keep the lids on tight."

The next night I woke up. I looked at the clock that sits on top of the brick on my night table. It was 1 A.M.

Julian was asleep with his pillow over his head. I went down to the living room.

I found his book on top of the TV, open to a page on African safaris. I went down to the basement and got my dad's hammer. I took it and the book outside. The moon was not quite as big as the night before, but there was plenty of light for working.

Every few feet I mashed up small spots of sandy ground with the hammer. Then I rounded them out just right.

I stood up and compared them to the picture in Julian's book. They looked the way they were supposed to—just like zebra tracks. Zebras leave hoofprints like horses. Their tracks are deeper in the ground than raccoon tracks. That's why I used the hammer.

In the morning, Julian was so excited he was yelling.

"Mom and Dad!! Huey! Come look! There was a *zebra* here last night!"

We all ran outside. My dad studied Julian's book and the tracks.

"Hard to believe," my dad said,

"but it sure does look that way!"

"Could it have been a horse?" my mom asked.

"All the horses around here wear shoes," my dad said. "These tracks don't show shoe prints."

Gloria came over and saw the tracks. *"Ama-a-a-zing!"* she said.

She and Julian decided to make a zebra trap. They made the cage out of straight sticks tied together with rope. I brought them the rope from the basement.

"We should put a carrot in the cage to attract the zebra," Gloria said. So Julian did.

He asked permission to sleep on the front porch, so he could watch for the

zebra and catch it. Gloria got permission to
sleep over and help.

Julian asked if I wanted to sleep downstairs with them to watch for the zebra.
"We could take turns watching and sleeping," he said.

I said there wasn't room for three of us
on the porch. Besides, I was tired.

But in the night I woke up. I looked out
the bedroom window. The moon was not
as big or as bright as the night before. I
went to the basement and got a hammer,
a chisel, and a flashlight. I crossed the living room on silent feet and peeked out the
window to the porch.

Julian was on the floor in his sleeping
bag with his pillow over his head. Gloria

was sitting up with her back against the wall, facing the zebra cage. But her head was tipped over on her shoulder. She was asleep.

On tiptoe I went out on the porch. The porch has one board that squeaks. I didn't step on it. The tracking book just touched Julian's hand. I put the hammer, the chisel

and the flashlight under my left arm. I was scared I would drop them. I bent down. Very carefully, I reached out with my right hand. Very gently, I took the book. Julian and Gloria did not wake up.

I walked to the zebra cage. I set my tools down on the grass.

Carrots are one of my favorite foods. I picked up the carrot in the cage. I bit off half and ate it. I used the flashlight to check the rest of the carrot for tooth marks I had made on the other half. I worked on them with my fingernail to make them look bigger. Then I put the flashlight down and put the carrot back in the trap.

I used the hammer to make more zebra tracks—into the trap and back out again.

I checked them with the light from the flashlight. They were okay. When I finished, I found a fallen pine bough. I used it to brush out all my own tracks.

I went to the edge of the street. At the edge of the street there is a narrow, sandy place. There was room for some very good tracks. Elephant tracks!

Elephants are *really* heavy. Their tracks

sink in. I used the chisel to soften up the ground before I made the tracks with my hammer. I made fat, round tracks, with bumps for the toe marks—five each on the front feet and three on the back, just like the picture in Julian's book. Afterward, I shined the flashlight on them. They looked good.

"The zebra was here!" Gloria said in the morning. "He was *here*—but I fell asleep. Huey! You should have helped us watch for him!"

"I'm too little," I said. "I'm afraid of zebras."

Julian and Gloria took my mom and dad and me outside and showed us the tracks—and the marks in the carrot.

My dad studied the carrot. "Those are tooth marks all right," he said.

My mom took the carrot and examined it. "*Some* kind of tooth marks..." she said. "But—" She never finished what she was going to say, because Julian was shouting and pointing at the street.

"There're more tracks out here! HUGE ones!"

We all went running to see.

"They look big enough to be elephant tracks!" Gloria said.

My mom said, "What I don't understand is why all these animals are coming to our house. Do you have any ideas, Huey?"

Everybody looked at me. I had to say something.

"It's really strange!" I said.

I am a tracker and a scout. I am strong and I am silent. I know many things. But I keep them to myself.

My Trip to Africa

I looked up. The sky was blue,
perfectly blue. I wanted to know
why.

I went down to my dad's work-
shop in the basement. He was
working on Julian's bicycle.

"Why—" I began.

"Can it wait a minute, Huey?" my dad said. "I'm trying to figure this blamed thing out."

I went upstairs to the den. My mom was sitting at the desk.

"Mom, why is the sky—" I began.

"Oh, Huey!" my mom said. "I was adding numbers in my head for income tax, and now I have to start all over again!"

I went outside. Julian and Gloria were kneeling on the lawn, working on a new, improved zebra trap.

"Julian," I said, "why—"

"Look at this!" Julian interrupted. "We have the carrot partway under a rock. A rope is partway under the rock too. When the zebra picks up the carrot, he'll move the rock and loosen the rope. That will make the cage door fall shut—and we'll catch him!"

"What if the zebra is too smart?" I asked.

"What do *you* know about zebras?" Julian asked.

"A real zebra would kick that cage to pieces!" I said.

I went back into the house and dived onto the couch. I didn't want to know about the sky anymore.

It's not blue all the time, anyhow, I thought. *Most of the time it isn't. So who cares?*

I stared at the living room wall. It had

some interesting things on it—things from Africa my mom had hung up there—a straw hat from Ghana, with green and yellow designs in it; and a cloak from Mali with bright blue and orange and white stripes; and a walking stick from we're not sure exactly where, with the head of a lion carved on it.

I kept staring at the things. The things kept staring back at me—especially the lion's head on the walking stick. Pretty soon I realized something. I wanted to go to Africa. I wanted to see where the wild zebras are. If I lived in Africa, I would be happy.

I went into the kitchen and made three peanut butter sandwiches. I put them in a plastic bag and put the plastic bag in my backpack. Then I went back into the living room. I stood on a chair and got the hat, the cloak, and the walking stick off their hooks.

I put the hat on my head. It was too big, so I put the cloak over my head first, and then the hat on top of it. That way, it fit just fine. I tried holding the walking stick. It felt just right.

I went out the door. I passed right by Julian and Gloria. They were working so hard on the trap that they didn't even see me.

I went down the street. The hat was good. It kept the sun out of my eyes. The cloak was good too. It felt warm. And the walking stick was the best of all. It seemed to want to go places without my even moving it.

Once someone had carried it all over Africa. He had leaned on it when he was tired. He had used it to cross rivers. When he needed to, he had used it as a weapon.

Right where my hand held it, it was smooth and shiny. The African hand that used to hold it had polished it for me. If I held on to it and didn't let go, it would show me the way to Africa.

I walked eight blocks. I got to the mall where the gas station is. I know the man who works at the gas station. His name is George. I asked him the way to Africa. He pointed.

"It's east of here," he said. "But be careful of the traffic."

I walked the way he pointed—toward where the sun was coming from. I used my stick to climb the hill above the gas station. I know the man who works on people's lawns up there. His name is Oscar. He was planting tulips.

"That's a nice stick you've got. Nice hat and cape too," Oscar said.

"Thank you," I said. "Do you happen to know the way to Africa?"

Oscar pointed.

"It's west of here," he said. He was pointing me right back where I came from!

"George at the gas station just told me it's east," I said.

"You can get there going east too," Oscar agreed.

I kept going the way I had been going.

My legs were getting tired. I saw a woman sweeping her steps. I've seen her lots, but I don't know her name. She looks old and wise. She looked like she should know the way to Africa.

"It's south of here," she said. And she pointed. "South and east. Or, south and west. You could do north too—but that would mean crossing the polar icecap."

"Everybody keeps telling me a different way to Africa!" I said. "Somebody is telling me lies!"

"No," the woman said. "No, they're not. Look!" she said, and held her arms out in front of her, wide and curved.

"The world is round, like a ball," she said, "so there's more than one way to anywhere."

She drew paths in the air with her finger. She explained everything so well that I could imagine all the seas and mountains I would cross, and all the rounding I would do to get to Africa.

I thanked her.

"Good luck," she said. "The shortest way is about six thousand miles."

I turned south. My feet hurt a little, but I was happy. Because the whole world is connected. So even if it was a long way, I couldn't miss Africa. Even if I made a few mistakes, someday I would get there.

Big clouds formed in the sky. They looked like the walls and towers of the ancient palaces in Africa. They made me glad I was going there.

I got to the park where Julian and Gloria and I go sometimes. I went through the park to a big log we like to play on. I sat down.

Right in front of me was a tree. A dog

stuck his head out from behind it and looked at me.

He was little and thin, with brown eyes and a tail that curved like a question mark. He had a cut on one of his ears.

I called him.

"Here, boy!" I said.

He perked up his ears as far as they would perk, but he didn't come closer.

"I won't hurt you," I said.

He sat down. He looked like he was wondering if he should believe me.

My backpack was under my cloak. I took it off and got out my sandwiches. I held one out to the dog and said, "Food, boy!" but he still wouldn't come.

"I'll call you 'Spunky,'" I told him. "You're hungry—but you still won't come just because a stranger calls you. That's being *spunky*."

He looked like he understood.

I put the sandwich on the ground halfway between us. Spunky walked up to it. He ate it in a gulp and stood and looked at me.

I finished my own sandwich.

"Do you want to go to Africa, Spunky?" I asked.

His body looked like he was saying no. His eyes looked like yes.

"Come on, then," I said. I got up and started walking again. Spunky followed me, not too close behind.

It was beautiful and peaceful in the park. By the river, lots of yellow flowers were growing. I decided to pick some for my mother. She couldn't help it that she couldn't add when someone talked to her. Probably only a genius could do that.

Then I remembered I was going to Africa. I couldn't take her any flowers if I was going to Africa. I sat down to think. I took out my last sandwich. I ate half and threw half to Spunky. He caught it in his mouth.

"We're going to Africa," I said. "But we don't need to go right away. We can go later. When we're older. When I have hiking boots."

I picked some of the flowers for my mother. I found a special stone to show my dad and Gloria. And Julian, maybe.

"Spunky," I asked, "do you want to come with me to my house?"

Spunky cocked his head as if he was deciding something. Then he followed me.

When we got close to home, I could hear voices calling me. My mom's, my dad's, Julian's, Gloria's. In the distance I could hear Gloria's mom and dad too, calling "HUUU-EY! HUUU-EY!"

Spunky looked at me and sat down by the driveway. I walked closer to the house. My mom had her back to me. She was shading her eyes from the sun and looking into the hedge.

"Come out, Huey!" she shouted. "This is *not* a joke!" She sounded worried.

I came up behind her.

"Here I am!" I said. I handed her my flowers.

She didn't even look at them, she just held them upside down with the stems squeezed tight in her hands.

"Huey!" she said. "Where *were* you? You know you're not supposed to go anywhere unless you tell us first!"

"You were busy and Dad was busy," I said.

"We are never *that* busy!" my mom said. "We need to know where you are."

I saw my dad down the street. He saw me and waved to Gloria and her mom and dad. They all came running up, out of breath and upset-looking.

"Huey!" my dad said. "Do you know how long you were away?"

"I don't know," I said. "I was going

to Africa, but I decided I didn't need to go right now. So I'm back."

"Huey," my dad said. "You must *never* do this again. Most people are nice, but some aren't. You could be in a dangerous place and not know it. A bad person could just reach out and grab you and that could be the end of you. No trip to Africa. Not even a trip home."

"I didn't go close to anyone," I said. "If anybody had tried to grab me, I would have run and screamed."

My dad stood over me and held me by the shoulders. "Next time you *ask* before you go somewhere!" he roared.

"Yes, sir!" I said.

Spunky barked. He was watching Dad and me. He had his two front feet on our lawn and his two back feet in the street. He looked like he was worried about what Dad would do to me.

"That's Spunky," I said. "He's my friend. I met him in the park and he came back with me. I don't think he has a home."

"And you want him to live with us?" my mom said.

"Yes," I said.

Everybody looked at Spunky. "He looks to be abandoned," Gloria's dad said. "Skinny. No collar."

"Can we keep him?" Julian said.

My mom and dad looked at each other.

"We'll have to call the animal shelter first," Mom said. "We have to make sure no one lost him."

"I'll call," I said.

Julian stayed out on the lawn with Spunky, so he wouldn't go away. The rest of us went into the house and I called. Nobody had lost a dog that looked like Spunky.

"If nobody shows up to claim him, you can keep him," Dad said. "But if you *ever* go off without telling us, he's going to the animal shelter. And he won't be coming back."

"I'll remember," I said. "I won't go any-place without telling you."

So that's the way it was. We persuaded Spunky to come in the house and eat. And he stayed.

My mom put eggs in his food, and his coat got shiny. And now he trusts us. He's

my dog and Julian's and partly Gloria's too. But mostly, he's mine. I'm the one who found him. I'm the one who named him.

When I feel bad, I can tell him things I can't even tell Gloria. When I'm sad, he puts his head on my arm and licks my hand. He makes a little moan in his throat and shows by his eyes that he understands.

The cloak and the hat and the walking

stick are back on the wall. I'm glad they went on a trip with me. Things like to be used.

The world is a lot, lot bigger than I ever knew. And sometimes, I know, it can be dangerous. But it's beautiful too. And someday I will go to Africa.

P. S.

Julian hadn't found any more tracks. He really, really wanted to see a zebra or an elephant. He got the idea that if we had a tree house, we could stay out of sight and watch for wild animals from above. So my dad helped us make a tree house in the pine tree in front of the house. It has a big platform, big enough for all of us—Julian and me and Gloria—to lie on. It has steps up the trunk that you can climb to get to it. And it has a special rope ladder you can climb too.

One day Julian figured out how to get Spunky up there by putting him in a basket that we hauled up with a rope and a pulley. I think Spunky liked being with us, even though he thought it was a long way off the ground.

Once we got him up in the tree house, Julian started wondering.

"Maybe it's because of Spunky that the animals don't come around anymore," he said. "Maybe they smell him and are scared of him."

I wasn't going to say anything. I am a

tracker and a traveler and a scout. I am silent. But I couldn't stand to be silent anymore.

"Julian," I said, "*I* was the raccoon. *I* was the zebra. *I* was the elephant."

And I explained it all.

Julian got very angry.

"Why did you do that to me?" he said.

"Because of the way you treat me," I said. "You treat me like I'm little and can't do anything. I decided to show what I can do."

"It was a great trick!" Gloria said. "Huey isn't a little kid. And Julian, you deserved it."

Julian still looked mad. "You aren't a little kid," Julian said. "You're smart. But don't do that to me again!"

"If you don't treat me bad, I won't trick you," I said.

Since then, Julian and I are friends. He even showed me everything in the tracking book, and read long parts to me—parts about the habits of animals, like how they like to come to water holes at dusk.

The three of us read that together, and it gave us the idea of making a water hole under the tree house. We put a big tub of water down there and a smaller, shallow one. We fill them with fresh water every afternoon. Then we go up into the tree house to watch for animals.

So far some birds have come and taken big, splashy baths in the shallow tub. Gloria's mom says if she helps out at home, Gloria can take some binoculars up to the tree house so we can see the birds even closer. My dad says he'll get us a book and an audiotape so we can identify different kinds of birds—and get them to come to us by copying their songs. He said he met a man once who had studied birds his whole life. He knew how to call hundreds of different birds that way. He would just make one or two calls, and out of nowhere, dozens of birds would come flying to him. Maybe one day we can do it.

My dad says if anybody finds wild animals around here, it'll be us.

I think he's right.

About the Author

Ann Cameron is the bestselling author of many popular books for children, including *The Stories Julian Tells*, *More Stories Julian Tells*, and *The Stories Huey Tells*. Her other books include *Julian, Dream Doctor; Julian, Secret Agent; Julian's Glorious Summer;* and *The Most Beautiful Place in the World*. Ms. Cameron lives in Guatemala.

You can visit Ann Cameron's Web site at www.childrensbestbooks.com.

Don't miss the next book about Huey!

More Stories Huey Tells

The top of the ladder looked a long way down. I thought of saying I wouldn't go down—but if I did, they'd all think I was scared.

Julian told me not to look at the bottom of the mine, just to lie on the ground and dangle my legs down toward the ladder and they'd let me down. I let myself off the edge of the mine and the rope pulled tight. I heard Spunky start whining and barking and Julian telling him to be quiet. But it was only a few seconds before I felt my feet on the ladder, and I climbed down it to the bottom of the mine.

Do you like funny stories?
You may also want to read . . .

MIAMI
Sees It Through

by Patricia & Fredrick McKissack

Then I hear Miss Spraggins saying, "What about you, Michael Andrew? Do you understand?"

"No, Ma'am," I say. Now, I'm meaning, *No, please don't call me Michael Andrew,* but she's thinking I'm saying, *No, I don't understand.*

Miss Spraggins is not with me on this. "I see," she says. "So you're a smarty-mouth. Then see if you can understand this. Michael Andrew, you have detention."

"What? But—"

"Not another word, young sir."

Who's ever heard of getting detention on the first day of school? I've got a sinking feeling—fourth grade is busted!

**Do you like stories with magic in them?
Try reading**

by Mordicai Gerstein

Martin got closer and saw the fox's ear twitch at a gnat. He got closer still and could see every gleaming hair in the fox's gold-orange coat. And when Martin was close enough to touch the fox's tail with a broomstick (if he'd had one), a stream crossed the path and the fox stopped. Martin, taken by surprise, almost tripped over the fox's tail.

The fox turned and saw Martin. It didn't run. The fox stood in the path and looked directly into Martin's eyes.

Martin remembered Aunt Zavella's warning about looking into the eyes of a fox. *It's probably*, he thought, *just some Old Country superstition. What could possibly happen?*

SEVEN FAMOUS

GREEK PLAYS

SEVEN
FAMOUS
GREEK
PLAYS

EDITED, WITH INTRODUCTIONS, BY

Whitney J. Oates

ANDREW FLEMING WEST PROFESSOR OF CLASSICS,
PRINCETON UNIVERSITY, AND

Eugene O'Neill, Jr.

The Modern Library · New York

w

THE MODERN LIBRARY
is published by RANDOM HOUSE, INC.

Manufactured in the United States of America by H. Wolff

PREFACE

THE aim of this volume is to provide students and general readers with a representative selection of the extant Greek drama in the best available translations.

Every effort has been made to impress upon the reader the extreme importance of the musical element in the Greek plays. To accomplish this end, all choral or singing passages in the prose versions have been indented, and broken up into their various choric constituents. Likewise, speeches which are attributed to the Chorus in the manuscripts, if they are written in the regular meter of the dialogue passages, have been assigned to the Leader of the Chorus, who thus becomes almost another member of the cast. Furthermore, all passages which were sung or chanted, so far as can be determined by their meter in the original, have been so indicated in the present text.

The General Introduction attempts to present certain material, both historical and systematic, which is requisite to the understanding of the plays. It treats, for example, such subjects as the nature of the Greek theater, Greek Tragedy and Greek Comedy in general, and the lives and works of the individual dramatists. Accompanying each play is a short special introduction to that play, designed primarily to facilitate its understanding on the part of the reader. Each play also is accompanied by notes which endeavor to explain particular passages which otherwise might prove difficult to apprehend. A Glossary renders unnecessary a number of specific notes on the individual plays. It is hoped that the Glossary will prove a useful and valuable adjunct to the book.

The editors together assume the responsibility for the selection of translations. Mr. Oates edited the text and prepared the individual introductions for the plays of Aeschylus, Sophocles and Euripides. He also prepared that part of the General Introduction which deals with tragedy and the tragedians. Mr. O'Neill edited the text, revised the translation, and prepared the introduction for the play by Aristophanes, as well as that portion of the General Introduction which deals with comedy and the comic poets. He likewise compiled the Glossary.

The resources of the two-volume Random House edition of *The Complete Greek Drama*, which contains all of the surviving forty-seven plays written by Aeschylus, Sophocles, Euripides, Aristophanes and Menander, were drawn upon for this collection. The editors earnestly hope that this volume will further the understanding and appreciation of these masterpieces of Greek creative art.

WHITNEY J. OATES
EUGENE O'NEILL, JR.

CONTENTS

CONTENTS

GENERAL INTRODUCTION

I. Tragedy

THE plays of Aeschylus, Sophocles and Euripides were written during the fifth century B.C. Behind them lies a rich literary and dramatic, or at least quasi-dramatic, tradition, which accounts in no small measure for the depth, scope and complexity of the art form which the plays embody. The problem of fully understanding the dramas is therefore not a simple one, since they cannot be divorced completely from the epic, lyric, and dramatic tradition which precedes them.

By far the most important factor in the tradition is the epic which we know chiefly through the *Iliad* and the *Odyssey*. In the interval between the epics of Homer, which scholars date variously from the tenth to the eighth century B.C., and the age of the three great tragic poets, thinkers began to explore the various phenomena of the external world and came to understand many aspects of nature which had hitherto been shrouded in complete mystery. The creative literary activity of this epoch likewise betokens on the part of the Greeks an increasingly higher level of self-understanding and self-consciousness, in the best sense of the word. At this time appeared a group of lyric poets, who had looked deeply within their own natures, and through the vehicle of their poetry made abundantly evident how thoroughly they understood the essential character of man's inner being. In Greek tragedy as we now have it we meet a fully developed dramatic form.

THE THEATER

It is absolutely necessary for anyone who desires to apprehend as completely as possible these Greek plays, to re-create them imaginatively as dramas, that is, as actual plays, produced dramatically before an audience. A spectator of a Greek dramatic performance in the latter half of the fifth century B.C. would find himself seated in the *theatron,* or *koilon,* a semicircular, curved bank of seats, resembling in some respects the closed end of a horseshoe stadium. He has climbed up the steps (*klimakes*) to reach his seat, which is in a section (*kerkis*). Probably he has in the process walked along the level aisle (*diazoma*) which divides the lower and the upper parts of the *theatron.* Below him, in the best location in the theater, is the throne of the priest of Dionysus, who presides in a sense over the whole performance, which is essentially religious in character. The *theatron* is large—in fact, the one in Athens, in the Theater of Dionysus, with its seats banked up on the south slope of the Acropolis, seated approximately 17,000 persons.

The spectator sees before him a level circular area called the *orchestra,* in the center of which stands an altar, which figures frequently as a stage-property in a number of the plays. A part of the dramatic action will take place in the *orchestra,* as well as the manoeuvres and dance figures performed by the Chorus as they present their odes. To the right and left of the *theatron* are the *parodoi,* which are used not only by the spectators for entering and leaving the theater, but also for the entrances and exits of actors and the Chorus.

Directly beyond the circular *orchestra* lies the *skene* or scene-building. In most plays the *skene* represents the façade of a house, a palace, or a temple, and normally had three doors which served as additional entrances and exits for the actors. Immediately in front of the scene-building **was a** level platform, called the *proskenion* or *logeion,* where much of the dramatic action of the plays takes place. Flanking the *proskenion* were two projecting wings, the so-called *paraskenia.*

Dramatic productions of the fifth century B.C. involved the use of two mechanical devices, with which the student of Greek drama should be familiar. One, the *eccyclema,* was developed in the fifth century. It was some kind of platform on wheels, which, so far as we can discover, was rolled out from the *skene,* and in this position was supposed to represent an interior scene. The other was the "machine." Frequently at the close of a play the dramatist introduced a god into the action, who would naturally be expected to appear from above. He apparently was brought in by some kind of crane or derrick, called the "machine." Inasmuch as the god who was thus introduced usually served to disentangle the complicated threads of the dramatic action, and on occasions seemed to be brought in quite gratuitously by a playwright unable to work out a dénouement from elements already in the situation, the term *deus ex machina,* "the god from the machine," has become standard in dramatic criticism.

THE PERFORMANCE

In Athens of the fifth century B.C. dramas were presented only on two occasions, both of which marked religious festivals. At other times plays were presented at rural festivals in various Greek communities, when the productions, so to speak, would "go on the road." In the city, the less important of the festivals, called the *Lenaea,* or Festival of the Wine-Press, was held in January/February of each year. The more important festival, however, was the so-called *Greater* **or** *City Dionysia,* which was celebrated annually in **March/**

April in honor of the god, Dionysus.[1] Large audiences attended the festival, and witnessed the various performances. Earlier in the century admission to the performances was free, but later the cost was two obols, which would be refunded by the State to anyone who could show legitimate need.

Three contests for poets were held in the *Greater Dionysia,* one in comedy, one in tragedy, and one in the dithyramb. Prior to the Peloponnesian War the festival apparently lasted six days. On the first took place the great ceremonial procession which was followed on the second by the competition for the dithyrambic choruses. The dithyramb was an elaborate choral ode sung and performed by a trained chorus of fifty, the song itself having a direct bearing upon the central religious orientation of the whole festival and its connection with the god, Dionysus. Ten dithyrambs were presented in the contest on this day. Five comic poets each submitted a play for the competition in comedy which occupied the third day. Three tragic poets each submitted a tetralogy for the contest in tragedy which filled the last three days of the festival. A tragic poet had to present a group of four plays, three of them tragedies, either on separate themes or all on the same subject, plus a somewhat lighter after-piece known as a satyr-play. During the days of the Peloponnesian War, 431-404 B.C., the festival was reduced from six to five days in length, and the number of

---

[1] Greek drama had a common close association with the spring festivals which were held to celebrate the worship of Dionysus. This god, as one of the Greek anthropomorphic divinities, symbolized the spirit of fertility, of generation and regeneration, which marks the season of spring, and he also came to be identified with the vine. Even in the fifth century the dramatic performances in the *Greater Dionysia* were still an integral part of a very elaborate religious service. The Theater of Dionysus in Athens lay within the sacred precinct of the god. The very altar in the center of the *orchestra* was not primarily a stage property, though the dramatists sometimes took advantage of its presence there, but it was a real religious altar. Behind the *skene* were temples dedicated to the god. Hence it is no wonder that the Greek drama tends to be more religious than secular.

comic competitors was diminished from five to three. During these years the program for the last three days contained a tragic tetralogy in the morning followed by a comedy in the afternoon.

Great care and expense went into the individual dramatic productions. The poet himself in many instances directed his own play, or even acted in it. In all probability he helped select his cast, all the parts of which were taken by male actors, coached them and supervised the training of the Chorus. Normally in the tragedies there were not more than three actors for each play, any one of whom might take more than one part if the exigencies of the piece demanded it. A wealthy citizen stood the cost of a play's production, a responsibility which was placed upon him by the State, and was regarded as a legitimate obligation of his position and citizenship.

The tragedies combined within them many variegated elements: rhythm in the poetry, vivid action, and brilliant color. There was also solo and choral singing, plus a strikingly posed and highly stylized dancing. A further effect was added by the fact that the actors all wore masks. This may have been partially because the audience was so far removed from the actors that it was impossible to achieve any effects through facial expressions.

THE STRUCTURE OF THE TRAGEDY

The typical Greek tragedy is divided into certain definite parts. The play opens with a *prologue,* a scene in which a single character may speak, or a dialogue may take place. In general in this short introductory scene, the poet acquaints the audience with the requisite information concerning the dramatic situation of the play.

After the *prologue* comes the *parodos,* the first appearance of the Chorus. The members of this group enter the *orches-*

tra, singing and dancing, clearly suiting the rhythm of their motion and their gesticulations to the gravity and import of the words they sing. As time passes in the fifth century the Chorus in tragedy steadily diminishes in importance. In Euripides, particularly in his later plays, the Chorus merely sings lyrical interludes which have little or no coherence with the play. Normally the members of the Chorus serve as interested commentators upon the action, sometimes functioning as a background of public opinion against which the situation of the particular play is projected, or again becoming the vehicle whereby the poet is able to make clearer the more universal significance of the action. At the conclusion of the *parodos,* the Chorus almost always remains "on stage" throughout the remainder of the play. In the tragedies there are usually fifteen members in the Chorus. One of this number normally acts as a leader who may do solo singing and dancing, or may become virtually another character in the *dramatis personae.* Sometimes the Chorus breaks into two groups which sing responsively.[2]

As soon as the opening choral song has been completed, there comes the first *episode.* This is the exact counterpart of the act or scene in a modern play. A *stasimon* or choral ode succeeds the *episode* and the remainder of the piece is made up of these two parts in alternation. A normal play contains four or five of each. On occasion a *commus* takes the place of a *stasimon.* The *commus* is a lyric passage, sung by an actor or actors together with the Chorus. Intricate meters distinguish the *stasimon* and *commus,* whereas the spoken passages of dialogue or monologue in the *episodes* are written in the iambic trimeter, a close equivalent to the

---

[2]It is possible in translation to give only an incomplete impression of the highly complicated rhythmic and metric structure of the choral passages. Suffice it to say that they had a carefully articulated and balanced symmetry of constituent parts, for which there were certain flexible conventions. The *strophe* is balanced by the *antistrophe;* the pair is sometimes followed by an *epode.* This basic pattern is varied on occasion by the use of repeated refrains and similar devices.

iambic pentameter or blank verse in English. After the series of *episodes* and *stasima,* there is the finale or *exodus,* the closing scene of the play at the end of which the Chorus leaves the view of the audience by way of the *parodoi.*

ARISTOTLE ON TRAGEDY

The most important document to come out of antiquity concerning Greek tragedy is of course the justly famous *Poetics* of Aristotle. In it, though it was written some fifty years after the heyday of Greek tragedy, Aristotle devotes himself almost exclusively to this form of art.

Upon analysis Aristotle concludes that there are in tragedy six basic elements which he calls Plot, Character, Diction, Thought, Spectacle, and Song. However, preliminary to his whole study in the *Poetics,* he introduces the conception of *mimesis,* or "imitation," which Plato had already used before him, as fundamental to the phenomena of art. In saying that the artist "imitates" his models, Aristotle does not use the word in its primary sense of "copying," but rather is seeking to give a secondary meaning to the term. By the word he seems to mean the process which takes place when an artist creates his work of art. It is through *mimesis* that form comes to be imposed upon the artist's material, broadly conceived. Aristotle insists that "poetry is something more philosophic and of graver import than history, since its statements are of the nature of universals, whereas those of history are singulars." Hence poetry "imitates" universals, and the process of *mimesis* produces a resultant work of art in which the "universal" aspect constitutes the very essence. Aristotle classifies the six basic elements according to the rôle each of them occupies in the process of artistic "imitation." He maintains that Diction and Song refer to the medium of "imitation," Spectacle to the manner of "imitation," while Plot, Character, and Thought refer to the objects of "imitation." Of the six elements Aristotle holds that Plot is the most important, with Character second.

An acquaintance with these six elements and with the Aristotelian conception of *mimesis* are necessary preliminaries to an understanding of his famous definition of tragedy: "Tragedy, then, is an imitation of an action that is serious, complete, and of a certain magnitude; in language embellished with each kind of artistic ornament, the several kinds being found in separate parts of the play; in the form of action, not of narrative; through pity and fear effecting the proper purgation of these and similar emotions." Aristotle's analysis and definition contain much that is valuable for one who is endeavoring to comprehend the inner nature of Greek tragedy. First, in his analysis of the elements he has shown that the dramatic synthesis is rich and complicated. He likewise properly emphasizes the elements of Plot and Character. Second, in the definition he insists upon its essential seriousness, its completeness, that is, its unity as an artistic whole, and its "magnitude," that is, its scale and elevation, which in some way raises it above the ordinary run of things human. Furthermore, he indicates what he believes the function of tragedy to be, the *catharsis*, or "proper purgation" of pity, fear, and similar emotions.

One more conception of Aristotle in the *Poetics*, his theory of the ideal tragic hero and the "tragic flaw," merits our attention. Aristotle says that tragedy must involve a change of fortune for a character, but this personage cannot be a completely virtuous man passing from fortune to misfortune, because this would be simply odious to the spectator. Nor can it involve a bad man passing from misery to happiness, because this would outrage our human feelings, our moral sense, and accordingly no appropriate tragic emotions would be aroused within us. Nor again can it involve a bad man passing from happiness to misery. Perhaps this would satisfy the moral sense, but it again would not arouse in us the appropriate tragic emotions. Hence Aristotle defines the

ideal tragic hero in these words: "A man who is highly re-
nowned and prosperous, but one who is not pre-eminently
virtuous and just, whose misfortune, however, is brought
upon him not by vice and depravity but by some error of
judgment or frailty."

There are several points to be particularly noted concerning Aristotle's conception of tragedy. First of all, he emphasizes the human element and insists implicitly that tragedy
involves human beings. Second, he emphasizes the single
individual in his argument concerning the tragic hero. Furthermore, he recognizes in human life states of happiness
and misery, fortune and misfortune, in and out of which
men pass. Here also he both implicitly and explicitly rejects
the mechanical conception of "poetic justice," that the good
prosper and the evil suffer. Aristotle likewise assumes the
existence of some kind of moral order in the universe, as
well as, by implication, the element of chance or luck, which
may be possibly extended to include fate or destiny. In summary, then, for Aristotle tragedy is serious and elevated. It
involves emotions of a particular sort. It looks at man and
his states, in a world in which there is an element of chance
or fate, but in which, at least so far as man himself is con-
cerned, there is a definite moral order in some sort, and not
moral chaos.

AESCHYLUS

Of the many writers of Greek tragedy only Aeschylus,
Sophocles, and Euripides are represented in the plays which
have survived. Aeschylus, the earliest of the three, was born
of a rather prominent family in Athens in 525 B.C., at a
time long before the city had achieved much distinction
among the peoples of the Greek area.

Aeschylus first competed in the dramatic contests in
Athens in 499 B.C. He achieved his first victory in 484 B.C.

and continued from then on to be highly successful in the theater. Aside from his dramatic activity, he apparently gained distinction in military affairs, having fought both at Marathon and Salamis. In all, he wrote approximately ninety plays, of which only seven have survived. We are told that he won first prizes in competition on thirteen occasions, his last victory occurring in 458 B.C. with his great trilogy, the *Oresteia*. He died in 455 B.C. while in Sicily, where he had gone shortly after his final tragic competition.

The loftiness of Aeschylean language and imagery is most notable, even though on some occasions the poet comes dangerously near bombast, a fact on which Aristophanes capitalized with great comic effect in *The Frogs*. However, Aeschylus' images possess a poetic depth and intensity which could only come from a mind driving deeply into the essence of that which it was seeking to express. Aeschylus' primary interest is in religion and theology. To be sure, he considers human phenomena, but not on the human level, or as ends in themselves. Aeschylus rather studies human affairs as means of throwing light upon the problems of religion and theology, which he considered more universal and more significant.

EURIPIDES

For general purposes of exposition it seems best to pass by Sophocles for the moment and turn to Euripides, who in many ways lies at the opposite extreme from Aeschylus in his basic interests. Euripides was born between the years 485 and 480 B.C. During his lifetime Euripides presented approximately eighty-eight plays, though he wrote in all about ninety-two. In the contests he was successful only four times, probably because his somewhat new and unorthodox views did not find immediate favor with the public. Certainly there is a strong strain of scepticism in his writing, and one becomes aware of the increasing doubt and uncertainty which pervade the plays, particularly those written towards the close of the Peloponnesian War, when Athens, the great city of ante-bellum days, was tottering upon the brink of ruin. Though Euripides' plays were not well received during his life, it is evident that after his death, during the fourth century B.C. and later, he was by far the most popular of the three tragedians. Euripides left Athens for the court of King Archelaus of Macedonia in about 408 B.C. and died there in 406 B.C.

Euripides' greatest claims to fame rest on his superb studies of human problems considered on the human level, his penetrating psychological analyses of his characters, his capacity to create genuine pathos, his sense of the dramatic possibilities of an individual scene, and his ability by means of dramatic innovations to reinterpret the traditional legends upon which all the dramatists relied for their material.

Euripides had a profound influence upon the drama. He seems to have shaken the domination which the traditional sagas exerted upon the playwrights; he reduced the importance of the Chorus, until it only served to provide lyric interludes between actual dramatic scenes, but above all he raised to supreme importance the study of character. Unlike Aeschylus he is not predominantly interested in religion and theology, but rather in ethical problems, in human beings face to face with the pain and evil of human life, as they exhibit now strength and now pathetic weakness. Although he never consistently formulates his ideas concerning the gods or the superhuman elements in the universe, he nevertheless seems to believe that they exist and are relevant to human life in some way or other.

SOPHOCLES

There remains to consider Sophocles, the great mediating figure between Aeschylus and Euripides. He was born about

495 B.C., some ten years or so before the birth of Euripides,
and lived to the great age of ninety, when he died about 405
B.C., surviving his younger contemporary by approximately
a year. The poet's family was wealthy, and he himself served
in public office on several occasions. In the main, however,
he devoted himself completely to the theater and in all wrote
about one hundred twenty-five plays of which now there are
but seven extant, and unfortunately none of these derives
from the first twenty-five years of his creative activity. His
plays met with wide popular success, as is indicated by his
twenty victories in tragic competition. Unlike Euripides,
who, as we have already noted, became bitterly disillusioned
towards the end of his life, and whose works show evidence of
this change of temper, Sophocles in his plays seems to main-
tain a consistent and firm approach to the problems of
tragedy.

Sophocles' mastery of dramatic technique is apparent in
all his plays, most notably, of course, in *Oedipus the King*.
Likewise in this tragedy, he demonstrated his ability to use
with overwhelming effectiveness the device of dramatic
irony. But his greatest excellence clearly lies in his general
view of life, which can scarcely be communicated in the
necessarily conceptual terms of criticism. It is, however, most
clearly expressed in two great choral odes, one on the wonders of man in the *Antigone* and the other on the laws of
Heaven in *Oedipus the King*. In the first of these Sophocles
eloquently asserts the dignity, worth and value of man, even
though there is death that he cannot conquer. In the second
the poet proclaims his belief in a mysterious and powerful
force behind the universe which sets and ordains the eternal
laws of the world, which are holy, though ultimately in-
comprehensible to man. These seem to be the two fundamental aspects of Sophocles' view of life: man the marvel working out his own destiny, making his own choices, but under
the guidance of Heaven and its everlasting laws. Sophocles
concentrates on the continual interaction of these two as-

pects. So struggles Oedipus, who has transgressed unwittingly a law of Heaven, but who through iron and inflexible will endeavors to work out his destiny and to assume his responsibility in a world in which human and divine elements are wholly interfused.

We have maintained that Aeschylus' basic orientation was towards theology and religion. On the other hand, we have insisted that Euripides was predominantly interested in human beings, on the human level, in their psychological states as they face the complex problems of human life. In a curious way Sophocles lies in a mean between these two poets, and seems to combine in himself their outstanding powers. He has the scale of Aeschylus plus Euripides' power of psychological analysis. He studies his human characters psychologically in their human environment, and yet he manages to approach the elevation of Aeschylus. He remains on the human level, yet always directs his gaze towards that which is superhuman. It is the miracle of Sophocles' genius which has enabled him to express this interpretation of life, so deep and comprehensive that it has rarely if ever been equalled in the creative literature of Western Europe.

W. J. O

II. Comedy

IN a number of its broadest aspects the comedy of the fifth century resembles tragedy. It was performed at festivals of Dionysus under the aegis of the Athenian state. Its expenses were met in the same manner as those of tragedy and the rivalry of the poets competing for the prizes was just as keen. It was performed in the same theater before the same type of audience, by a chorus of about the same size and by an equally limited number of actors. Its structure shows

xxii   *General Introduction*

many of the characteristic features of the mature tragic drama, such as *prologue, parodos,* and *exodus,* and the main body of both types of play consists of a series of relatively short scenes separated by choral interludes. The *prologues* of fifth-century comedy are not usually composed with much care or skill, and the situation is often explained to the spectators by one of the actors in a long and undramatic speech reminiscent of the Euripidean *prologue,* but we nowhere find a comic *prologue* consisting entirely of such a speech. The comic *parodos* is much more complicated and dramatic than the one usually found in the tragic play, and it contains peculiarities of form that are unknown in tragedy. The special interest of the comic *exodus* derives not from its form, which is quite free, but from its content. It is in the choral interludes between scenes that the unique features of the form and the structure of comedy are most evident. Whereas in tragedy these performances of the Chorus, for all their differences in content and in meter, almost invariably have the standardized form of the *stasimon,* in comedy they exhibit astonishing variety and frequent specialization.

The typical fifth-century comedy falls into two well-defined parts, usually of more or less equal length. The first of these we find devoted to the creation of some incongruous situation, the second to the results of this, presented in a series of short scenes that have little dramatic coherence and no development.

The influence of tragedy on classic comedy is evident in the increasing preoccupation with subjects that are utopian or timeless, and the traditional satire on contemporary events and personages recedes more and more into the background. In the early fourth century we observe what appears to be a sudden decline in the importance of the Chorus. In the New Comedy (after 340 B.C.) the Chorus is merely an adventitious band of revellers which entertains the audience between the acts into which the plays of this period are divided.

ARISTOPHANES

As is so often the case with ancient writers, we know next to nothing about the life of Aristophanes. Born about 445 B.C. in Attica, he began to write when he was very young, and his first play was produced when he was eighteen. He composed about forty comedies in all, but we do not know how often he was victorious. On several occasions he brought out his plays under other names, but we do not know why he did this. The date of his death is uncertain, but it must have been later than 387 B.C.

There has never been anything quite like the comic drama of Aristophanes, and regrettably there will never be anything quite like it again. The effect of the initial impact of these plays is one of bewilderment. One rubs one's eyes and wonders whether it really can have happened. A closer acquaintance and a bit of sober reflection disclose a number of distinct reasons for astonishment. The first of these is the absolute freedom of speech which the comic poet of the fifth century enjoyed. He might make fun, banteringly or bitterly, thoroughly and repeatedly, of anything; no person, no institution, no god, enjoyed the slightest vestige of immunity, and the Athenian populace seems to have enjoyed these libels and slanders so hugely that they did not even require that they be always amusing.

Equally astonishing is the pervading obscenity, so abundant and so varied that it cannot be ignored or excised. It is so closely interwoven into almost every part of these plays that to expurgate is to destroy. A bowdlerized Aristophanes may offer a selection of passages well adapted to teach Attic Greek to schoolboys, but it is not Aristophanes. There is no escaping the fact that Aristophanes wrote just as obscenely as he could on every possible occasion. If we would appreciate him properly we should bear this in mind and endeavor to cultivate the same attitude that he had; the most un-healthy approach is the denial of the obvious in the name of healthiness.

The distinguishing characteristic of Aristophanes is his brilliant insouciance. Endowed by nature with an intellect of an exceptionally high order and an imagination inexhaustibly fertile, he exercised his talents in a medium ideally suited to them. His best comedies are concatenations of splendid and dazzling conceits which follow one another in breathless abundance. He is never at a loss what to invent next; indeed, he hardly ever has time fully to exploit the humorous possibilities of one motif before he is occupied with another. A mind of this sort has no use for consistency, and that stodgy virtue may best be cultivated by the lesser talents, who need all the virtues they can get.

It is from this point of view that we must approach him if we would avoid misunderstanding him, and we must not forget that Plato adored him. He has naturally been mis-understood, grossly and variously. He has a lot to say about himself, but hardly a word of it can be taken seriously. This would be an easy deduction from the quality of his mind, but he repeatedly proves it by his actions, for he blandly denies doing what he plainly and frequently does. His views on political and social questions have been eagerly and pon-derously analyzed, but this is mostly a waste of time and energy. It is safe to say that whenever his wit is functioning properly we have no hope of discovering what his real feelings were.

Brilliance, however, was not his only gift, and his heart was as sensitive as his mind was keen. The soft side of his personality expresses itself in his lyrics, and here he astounds and delights us, at one moment with idyllic songs of the countryside, at another with lines of infinite tenderness and sympathy, particularly towards old men. Often in the midst of a lyric passage of great warmth and beauty something will touch off his wit, and a sentence that has begun in a gentle and sympathetic spirit will end with a devastating personal gibe or an uproarious bit of obscenity. The two sides of the poet's nature are not really separable; he can be both witty and lyrical, almost at one and the same moment. This strange and perfect blend of characteristics apparently so incompatible makes Aristophanes a wonderful man to read, and we begin to understand why Plato loved the old rogue as he did.

E. O'N., Jr.

BIBLIOGRAPHY

C. M. Bowra, *Sophoclean Tragedy*, Oxford, Clarendon Press, 1945

G. M. A. Grube, *The Drama of Euripides*, London, Methuen, 1941

A. E. Haigh, *The Tragic Drama of the Greeks*, Oxford, Clarendon Press, 1896

H. D. F. Kitto, *Greek Tragedy, A Literary Study*, London, Methuen, 1939

F. L. Lucas, *Euripides and his Influences*, Boston, Marshall Jones, 1923

G. Murray, *Aeschylus, The Creator of Tragedy*, Oxford, Clarendon Press, 1940

————, *Euripides and his Age*, New York, Holt, 1913

————, *Aristophanes: a Study*, Oxford, Clarendon Press, 1933

G. Norwood, *Greek Tragedy*, Boston, Luce, 1920

————, *Greek Comedy*, Boston, Luce, 1932

T. B. L. Webster, *Introduction to Sophocles*, Oxford, Clarendon Press, 1936

All the extant plays of ancient Greece can be found in *The Complete Greek Drama*, edited by Oates and O'Neill, New York, Random House, 1938

PROMETHEUS BOUND

by

AESCHYLUS

CHARACTERS IN THE PLAY

POWER
FORCE
HEPHAESTUS
PROMETHEUS
CHORUS OF THE DAUGHTERS OF OCEANUS
OCEANUS
IO
HERMES

INTRODUCTION

FEW GREEK tragedies present as many critical difficulties as does the *Prometheus Bound*. In the first place even its authenticity has been doubted, although this view has not commanded any general acceptance. Its date is likewise uncertain. Further, although the play is presumably one part of a trilogy, critics have not been able to determine with exactness what place it occupied in the larger dramatic unit and what was the content of its companion plays. Lastly, the question of its larger significance has provided ample material for critical debate.

So far as our information goes, we may with fair assurance accept the theory, now generally held, that the *Prometheus Bound* was the first play of the trilogy, followed by *Prometheus Unbound* and *Prometheus the Fire-Bearer*. In the trilogy the poet has treated in detail the legend of the great Titan, who took pity on the helplessness of men, and gave them the precious gift of fire which he stole from Heaven, wherewith they were able to improve their state and to learn the arts of civilization. Prometheus' theft contravened an ordinance of Zeus, the newly established Lord of Heaven, who had determined to destroy the race of men. Our play deals with Zeus' punishment of his rebellious subject, while the second of the series told of Prometheus' release, and the third, about which we have scarcely any knowledge, may have connected the legend with the institution of some religious festival of the Athenians.

In the *Prometheus Bound* Aeschylus was faced with a difficult problem of dramaturgy since he had to build a play

3

in which his central character could not move, in a very literal sense of the word. Consequently the poet found himself considerably limited in scope and was forced practically to eliminate from his play anything which we might call "action." Aeschylus solves the problem by introducing several characters who in one way or another set off the central figure. He contrasts Prometheus now with Oceanus, now with Io his fellow-sufferer at the hands of Zeus, and finally with Hermes, the "lackey of Zeus" as Prometheus bitterly calls him. In and through the dialogues between Prometheus and his various interlocutors gradually emerges the poet's analysis of the questions he is raising in the play.

Since we do not possess the rest of the trilogy, any attempt to give a general interpretation of the *Prometheus Bound* is hazardous. At least some points are certain. Here we have a play whose dramatic date lies almost at the beginning of mythological time. Furthermore, all the characters, save Io, are superhuman. Hence the poet has given the play a greater elevation than is to be found elsewhere in the extant Greek drama. Of course, he loses in "realism," but, to compensate this loss, he has put himself in a position whence he may appropriately attack the central problem which he has before him. This problem appears to be "What is the nature of the divine power which lies behind the universe? If that power is benevolent, beneficent or good, why is it that man suffers? Why is there evil in the world?" Our play seems to contain only the preliminaries to some kind of resolution of this most difficult of all philosophical and religious problems. Prometheus, the benignant, the "Suffering Servant," the benefactor of mankind, is posed against Zeus, the malignant tyrant, omnipotent, though not omniscient. A quasi-allegory or partial symbolism may be present here in this opposition between wisdom and brute force.

POWER

Dost thou shrink? Wilt thou groan for the foes of Zeus?
Take heed, lest thou groan for thyself.

HEPHAESTUS

Thou lookest upon a spectacle grievous to the eye.

POWER

I look upon one suffering as he deserves.—Now about his
sides strain tight the girth.

HEPHAESTUS

It must needs be done; yet urge me not overmuch.

POWER

Yet will I urge and harry thee on.—Now lower; with force
constrain his legs.

HEPHAESTUS

'Tis even done; nor was the labor long.

POWER

Weld fast the galling fetters; remember that he who ap-
praises is strict to exact.

HEPHAESTUS

Cruel thy tongue, and like thy cruel face.

POWER

Be thine the tender heart! Rebuke not my bolder mood,
nor chide my austerity.

HEPHAESTUS

Let us go; now the clinging web binds all his limbs.

(HEPHAESTUS *departs.*)

POWER

There, wanton, in thy insolence! Now for thy creatures of
a day filch divine honors. Tell me, will mortal men drain for
thee these tortures? Falsely the gods call thee Prometheus,

PROMETHEUS BOUND

(SCENE:—*A rocky gorge in Scythia.* POWER *and* FORCE
enter, carrying PROMETHEUS *as a captive. They are accompanied by* HEPHAESTUS.)

POWER

TO THIS far region of the earth, this pathless wilderness of
Scythia, at last we are come. O Hephaestus, thine is the
charge, on thee are laid the Father's commands in never-
yielding fetters linked of adamant to bind this miscreant to
the high-ridged rocks. For this is he who stole the flame of
all-working fire, thy own bright flower, and gave to mortal
men. Now for the evil done he pays this forfeit to the gods;
so haply he shall learn some patience with the reign of Zeus
and put away his love for human kind.

HEPHAESTUS

O Power and Force, your share in the command of Zeus
is done, and for you nothing remains; but I—some part of
courage still is wanting to bind with force a kindred god to
this winter-bitten gorge. Yet must I summon daring to my
heart, such dread dwells in the Father's word.—(*to* PROME-
THEUS) O high magnanimous son of prudent Themis, against
thy will and mine with brazen bonds no hand can loose I
bind thee to this unvisited lonely rock. No human voice will
reach thee here, nor any form of man be seen. Parched by
the blazing fires of the sun thy skin shall change its pleasant
hue; grateful to thee the starry-kirtled night shall come veil-
ing the day, and grateful again the sun dispelling the morn's

5

white frost. Forever the weariness of unremitting pain shall waste thy strength, for he is not born who can deliver thee. See now the profit of thy human charity: thou, a god not fearing the wrath of the gods, hast given to mortal men honors beyond their due; and therefore on this joyless rock thou must keep vigil, sleepless and weary-clinging, with un-bended knees, pouring out thy ceaseless lamentations and unheeded cries; for the mind of Zeus knows no turning, and ever harsh the hand that newly grasps the sway.

POWER

It may be so, yet why seek delay in vainly spent pity? Feel you no hatred for this enemy of the gods, who hath be-trayed to mortals your own chief honor?

HEPHAESTUS

Kinship and old fellowship will have their due.

POWER

'Tis true; but where is strength to disobey the Father's words? Fearest thou not rather this?

HEPHAESTUS

Ever merciless thou art, and steeped in cruelty.

POWER

It healeth nothing to weep for him. Take not up an idle burden wherein there is no profit.

HEPHAESTUS

Alas, my cherished craft, thrice hateful now!

POWER

Why hateful? In simple sooth thy art hath no blame for these present ills.

HEPHAESTUS

Yet would it were another's, not mine!

POWER

All toil alike in sorrow, unless one were lord none is truly free, save only Zeus.

HEPHAESTUS

This task confirms it; I can nothing deny.

POWER

Make haste then to bind him in fetters, lest the f. detect thee loitering.

HEPHAESTUS

Behold the curb; it is ready to hand.

POWER

Strongly with thy hammer, strongly weld it about his hands; make him fast to the rock.

HEPHAESTUS

The work goes on, it is well done.

POWER

Harder strike them, tighter draw the links, leave nothing loose; strange skill he hath to find a way where none ap-peared.

HEPHAESTUS

One arm is fastened, and none may loose it.

POWER

Fetter the other, make it sure; he shall learn how all his cunning is folly before Zeus.

HEPHAESTUS

Save now my art hath never wrought harm to any.

POWER

Now strongly drive the biting tooth of the adamantine wedge straight through his breast.

HEPHAESTUS

Alas, Prometheus! I groan for thy pangs.

the Contriver, for no cunning contrivance shall help thee to
slip from this bondage.

(POWER *and* FORCE *depart.*)

PROMETHEUS (*alone, chanting*)
O air divine, and O swift-wingèd winds!
Ye river fountains, and thou myriad-twinkling
Laughter of ocean waves! O mother earth!
And thou, O all-discerning orb o' the sun!—
To you, I cry to you; behold what I,
A god, endure of evil from the gods.

Behold, with what dread torments
I through the slow-revolving
Ages of time must wrestle;
Such hideous bonds the new lord
Of heaven hath found for my torture.
Woe! woe! for the present disasters
I groan, and for those that shall come;
Nor know I in what far sky
The dawn of deliverance shall rise.

Yet what is this I say? All future things
I see unerring, nor shall any chance
Of evil overtake me unaware.
The will of Destiny we should endure
Lightly as may be, knowing still how vain
To take up arms against Necessity.
Silent I cannot keep, I cannot tongue
These strange calamities. Lo, I am he
Who, darkly hiding in a fennel reed
Fountains of fire, so secretly purloined
And gave to be the teacher of all arts
And giver of all good to mortal men.
And now this forfeit for my sin I pay,
Thus lodged in fetters under the bare sky.

Woe's me!
What murmur hovereth near?
What odor, where visible shape
Is none? Some god, or a mortal,
Or one of the middle race?
Hath he come to this world's-end
Idly to gloat o'er my toils,
Or what would he have?—Behold me
Fettered, the god ill-fated,
The foeman of Zeus, the detested
Of all who enter his courts,
And only because of my love,
My too-great love for mankind.
Ah me! once more the murmur
I hear as of hovering birds;
And the air is whirring with quick
Beating of wings. For me
There is fear, whatever approaches.

(*The* CHORUS OF THE DAUGHTERS OF OCEANUS *enter, drawn in a winged car.*)

CHORUS (*singing*)

strophe I

Fear nothing; in friendship and eager
With wingèd contention of speed
Together we draw near thy rock.
Scarce we persuaded our father,
But now at last the swift breezes
Have brought us. Down in the depth
Of our sea-cave came the loud noise
Of the welding of iron; and wonderment
Banished our maiden shame;
All in haste, unsandalied; hither
We flew in this wingèd car.